Superphonics **Storybooks will help your child to learn to read using Ruth Miskin's highly effective phonic method. Each story is fun to read and has been carefully written to include particular sounds and spellings.**

The Storybooks are graded so your child can progress with confidence from easy words to harder ones. There are four levels - Blue **(the easiest),** Green**,** Purple **and** Turquoise **(the hardest). Each level is linked to one of the core** *Superphonics Books***.**

ISBN 0 304 80545 5

Text copyright © 2002 Gill Munton
Illustrations copyright © 2002 Sue King

Editorial by Gill Munton
Design by Sarah Borny

The rights of Gill Munton and Sue King to be identified as the author and illustrator of this Work have been asserted by them in accordance with the Copyright, Designs and Patents Act 1988.

First published in Great Britain 2002

10 9 8 7 6 5 4 3 2

First published in 2002 by Hodder Children's Books, a division of Hodder Headlir 338 Euston Road, London N

Reprinted in 2002

Printed in Hong Kor

A CIP record is regi

Target words

All the Blue Storybooks focus on the following sounds:

a as in **jam** | **e** as in **bed**
i as in **fish** | **o** as in **box**
u as in **mug** |

These target words are featured in the book:

at	rat a tat tat	dish
bath	tap	fish
can	that	his
cat		in
Chad	bed	jimjams
Dad('s)	Bev	Lin
Dan	Ed	with
fat	Ned	
ham	red	box
hat	Ted	choc(s)
jam		chop(s)
Mags	big	cot
Max	chip(s)	hot
	dip(s)	

lot(s)	hug	rub a dub
on	hum a dum	dub
pop(s)	dum	rug
Rob	jug	up
	mug	shush
bun(s)	Mum	tub
but	nut(s)	
chug a tug	pup(s)	
tug		

Other words

Also included are some common words (e.g. **and**, **like**) which your child will be learning in his or her first few years at school.

A few other words have been used to help the stories to flow.

Reading the book

1 Make sure you and your child are sitting in a quiet, comfortable place.

2 Tell him or her a little about the stories, without giving too much away:

In the first story, everyone is eating!

In the second story, Mum and Max are trying not to wake the baby ...

In the third story, three pups are keen to run away from their mum.

In the last story, a little girl is getting ready for bed.

This will give your child a mental picture; having a context for a story makes it easier to read the words.

3 Read the target words (above) together. This will mean that you can both enjoy the stories without having to spend too much time working out the words. Help your child to sound out each word (e.g. **b-o-x**) before saying the whole word.

4 Let your child read each of the stories aloud. Help him or her with any difficult words and discuss the story as you go along. Stop now and again to ask your child to predict what will happen next. This will help you to see whether he or she has understood what has happened so far.

Above all, enjoy the stories, and praise your child's reading!

Ruth Miskin's Superphonics

Blue Storybook

Fish
and Chips

by Gill Munton

Illustrated by Sue King

Hodder
Children's
Books

a division of Hodder Headline Limited

Fish and chips

Bev likes buns
 and chocs in a box.
Ed likes eggs and ham.

Chad likes chops
with chips in a dish.

Rob likes red, red jam.

Lin likes lots of lemon pops.

Ned likes nuts and dips.

Mags likes
mashed bananas ...

... but I like
fish and chips!

Shush!

Max was in bed.
Dan was in his cot.

"Mum!" called Max.

"Can I have
a mug of water?"

Mum came up
with the water.
"Shush!" she said.

"Mum!" called Max.
"Can I have my Ted?"

Mum came up with Ted. "Shush!" she said.

"Mum!" called Max.
"Can I have a hug?"

Mum came up and
gave him a hug.

"Atishoo!" she said.

"Shush!" said Max.

Rub a dub dub,
Three pups in a tub,

Chug a tug tug,

Two pups on a rug,

Rat a tat tat,

One pup in a hat,

Hum a dum dum,

No pups -
but one Mum!

Hot tap, cold tap,
Soap in a dish,

A fat cat,
And look at that!
A little red fish!

A water jug, Dad's mug,
A big fat ted,

On with the jimjams,

And into bed!